Me, Too!

by Lucinda Cotter

illustrated by Nadia Ronquillo

raintree

a Capstone company — publishers for children

Engage Literacy is published in the UK by Raintree.
Raintree is an imprint of Capstone Global Library Limited, a company incorporated in England and Wales having its registered office at 264 Banbury Road, Oxford, OX2 7DY – Registered company number: 6695582

www.raintree.co.uk

Illustration copyright Capstone/Nadia Ronquillo

Editorial credits
Marissa Kirkman, editor; Charmaine Whitman, designer; Katy LaVigne, production specialist

10 9 8 7 6 5 4 3 2
Printed and bound in India.

Me, Too!

ISBN: 978 1 4747 3913 9

Contents

Chapter 1
The copycat

"Mum, Rosie keeps copying me!" said Cam.
He sat at the kitchen table
and crossed his arms.

Just then, Rosie came in and sat next
to Cam.
She crossed her arms just like him.

"See," said Cam, pointing to his sister.
"She's a copycat!"

Rosie pointed right back at him.

"Mum, can you please tell her to stop?"

"She's only little," said Mum.
"You're her big brother, and she wants
to be like you."

"Well, it's making me angry," said Cam.

"Me, too!" said Rosie.

Rosie copied Cam all day.
When Mummy made cupcakes,
Cam said, "I like the lemon ones best."

"I do, too!" said Rosie.

"I've changed my mind," said Cam.
"I really like the chocolate ones best."

"Me, too!" shouted Rosie.

When Cam put his baseball cap on back to front, Rosie did the same with her cap.

When Cam went outside to ride his red scooter, Rosie followed.

When Cam bumped his knee on the table, he jumped up and down, holding his leg.

Rosie jumped up and down, too.

"You didn't even hurt yourself," said Cam.

"I did, too," whispered Rosie.

Chapter 2
The plan

Cam was fed up.
He had to find a way to stop Rosie
from copying everything he did.

At dinner, Cam asked for a big helping
of green beans.
He knew Rosie didn't like beans.
He looked at Rosie, picked up the beans
with his fork and quickly ate them.
"Yummy!" he said loudly.

But to Cam's surprise, Rosie picked up
a bean with her fork.
She bit straight into it.
"Yummy!" she said.

"Look at Rosie!" cried Mum.
"She's eating beans!
Good girl, Rosie!"

Cam couldn't believe it!

The next morning, Cam and Rosie
were playing in the park.
"I'm going to go down the big slide,"
said Cam.
He knew that Rosie was frightened
of going down the big slide.
So far, she hadn't been able to do it.

Cam slowly climbed the ladder.
He could see Rosie down below,
looking up at him with wide eyes.
There was no way she would follow him,
he thought.

He got to the top and pushed off.
He slid down and down, and around
and around.

But, when he got to the bottom,
Cam was surprised to see Rosie
coming down right behind him.

"Wow!" said Mummy.
"What a brave girl you are, Rosie!"

It was no use.
Whatever Cam did, Rosie did it, too.

Chapter 3
The visitor

The next day, Cam's best friend,
Anton, came over.

When Rosie came outside to watch
them play catch, Cam was embarrassed.
"Go away, Rosie," he said.
"Anton and I want to play by ourselves."

But to Cam's surprise, Anton said,
"I don't mind if Rosie wants to play, too."

Anton pushed his sleeves up.
"Here, catch!" he said.
He threw the ball to Rosie.

Rosie grinned.
She pushed her sleeves up, too.
"Catch!" she said.
She threw the ball back to Anton.

That day, they had soup for lunch.

"I'm really hungry!" said Anton.

"Me, too!" said Rosie.

"Yum! Chicken noodle!
My favourite," said Anton.

"Mine, too!" said Rosie.

"Hang on," said Cam.
"I thought tomato was your favourite,
just the same as me."

Rosie shook her head.
"Not anymore!" she said.

Chapter 4
A change of heart

Everywhere Anton went, Rosie went, too.

Everything Anton did, Rosie copied it.

She seemed to have forgotten all about Cam. It was as if she didn't know he was there!

Cam suddenly felt very left out.

When Rosie went to have her afternoon nap, Cam and Anton were finally by themselves.

"Does it bother you that my little sister hangs around and copies everything you do?" asked Cam.

"I don't mind.
I kind of like it," Anton smiled.
"I don't have any brothers or sisters.
It's nice to have someone who looks up
to me and thinks I'm cool.
You're really lucky, you know."

That evening, after Anton had gone home,
Cam sat next to Rosie on the sofa.
When he laughed at a cartoon on the TV,
Rosie laughed, too.

When he booed the bad guy, Rosie booed, too.

Cam looked at Rosie.
She was sitting just the same way he was.

"I'm glad you're my sister," he said.

"Me, too!" said Rosie.